A Beach Tail

Karen Lynn Williams

Illustrated by Floyd Cooper

BOYDS MILLS PRESS
Honesdale, Pennsylvania

Illustrator's Note
Special thanks to Rylee for a great job modeling as Gregory.
And thank you, Emma Grochowski, for the lion.
　　　　　　　　　　　　　—F.C.

Text copyright © 2010 by Karen Lynn Williams
Illustrations copyright © 2010 by Floyd Cooper

Boyds Mills Press, Inc.
815 Church Street
Honesdale, Pennsylvania 18431
Printed in China

Library of Congress Cataloging-in-Publication Data

Williams, Karen Lynn.
　A beach tail / Karen Lynn Williams ; illustrated by Floyd Cooper. —
1st ed.
　　p. cm.
　Summary: When his father tells him not to leave the lion he is drawing
on the beach, a little boy starts making a very, very long tail—and a trail
to follow back.
　ISBN 978-1-59078-712-0 (hardcover : alk. paper)
[1. Beaches—Fiction. 2. Drawing—Fiction. 3. Fathers and sons—
Fiction.]　I. Cooper, Floyd, ill. II. Title.
　PZ7.W66655Be 2010
　[E]—dc22
　　　　　　　　　　　　　　　　　2009035944

First edition
The text of this book is set in 22-point Adobe Caslon.
The illustrations are done in pastels.

10 9 8 7 6 5 4

In memory of my father, who took me to the beach
and held my hand in the waves
   —K.L.W.

For Kai
   —F.C.

Swish-swoosh

Gregory drew a lion in the sand.

"A Sea Lion?" Dad asked.
"A Sandy Lion," Gregory said.
"Sandy needs a tail," said Dad.
Gregory picked up his sturdy drawing stick.
"Don't go in the water,
and don't leave Sandy," Dad said.
"I won't," said Gregory.
Dad sat down on the dolphin towel
under the blue umbrella.

Swish-swoosh

Gregory drew a tail.
He did not go in the water,
and he did not leave Sandy.
Sandy's tail got longer until
Gregory came to a purple jellyfish.
He made a loop around the gooey blob.
So did Sandy's tail.

Swish-swoosh

Gregory came to the mound
of an old castle washed smooth by the waves.
He went up and over and down.
So did Sandy's tail.
But Gregory did not go in the water,
and he did not leave Sandy.

Sandy's tail got longer
until Gregory came to a horseshoe crab.
He made a big zig and then a zag
around that old crab's pointer.
Sandy's tail went zigzag, too.

Swish-swoosh

Gregory came to a giant hole.
Gregory went down and up.
So did Sandy's tail.

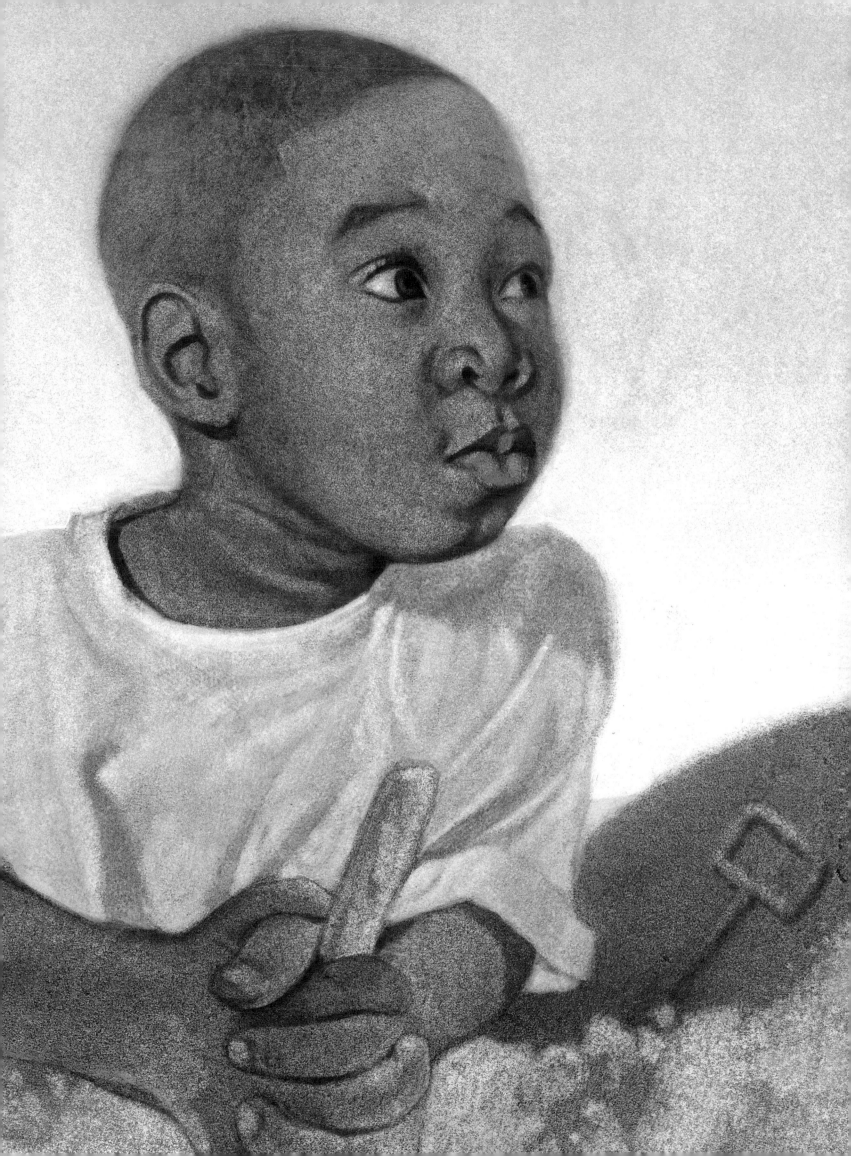

Sandy's tail got longer
until Gregory saw a tiny ghost crab
scurry sideways into his dark, round hole.
Gregory went round and round the hole.
Sandy's tail went round and round, too.
But Gregory did not go in the water,
and he did not leave Sandy.

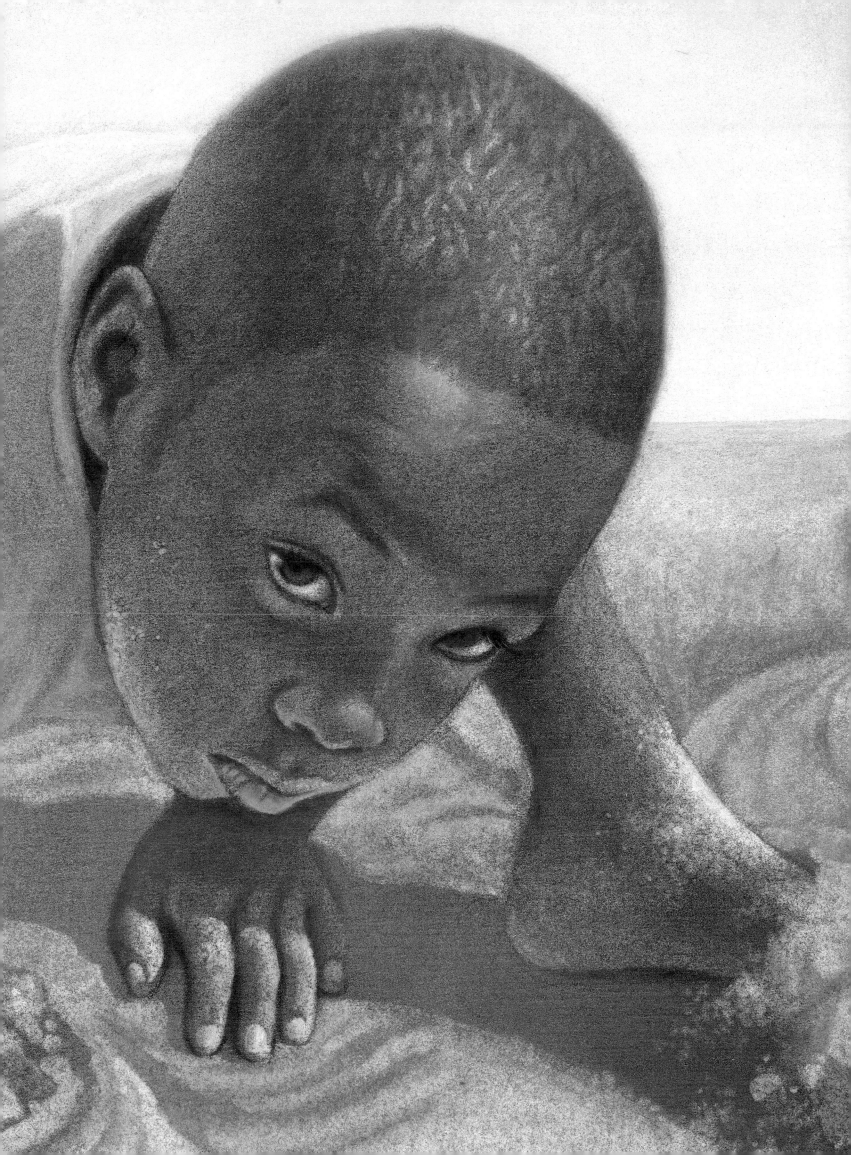

Swish-swoosh

Gregory wrote his nickname:
G-R-E-G.
Sandy's tail got longer.
Suddenly a wave snuck up onto the sand.
It tickled Gregory's toes.
Gregory jumped back
and traced the lacy wave line.
Sandy's tail made a wavy line, too.
But Gregory did not go in the water,
and he did not leave Sandy.

Swish-swoosh

Sandy's tail got longer
until Gregory came to a jetty.
He heard a loud *ROAR*.
Gregory looked up.
A giant wave crashed on the rocks.
The spray splashed Gregory.

He turned around
to look for Dad.
Uh-oh.
What now?

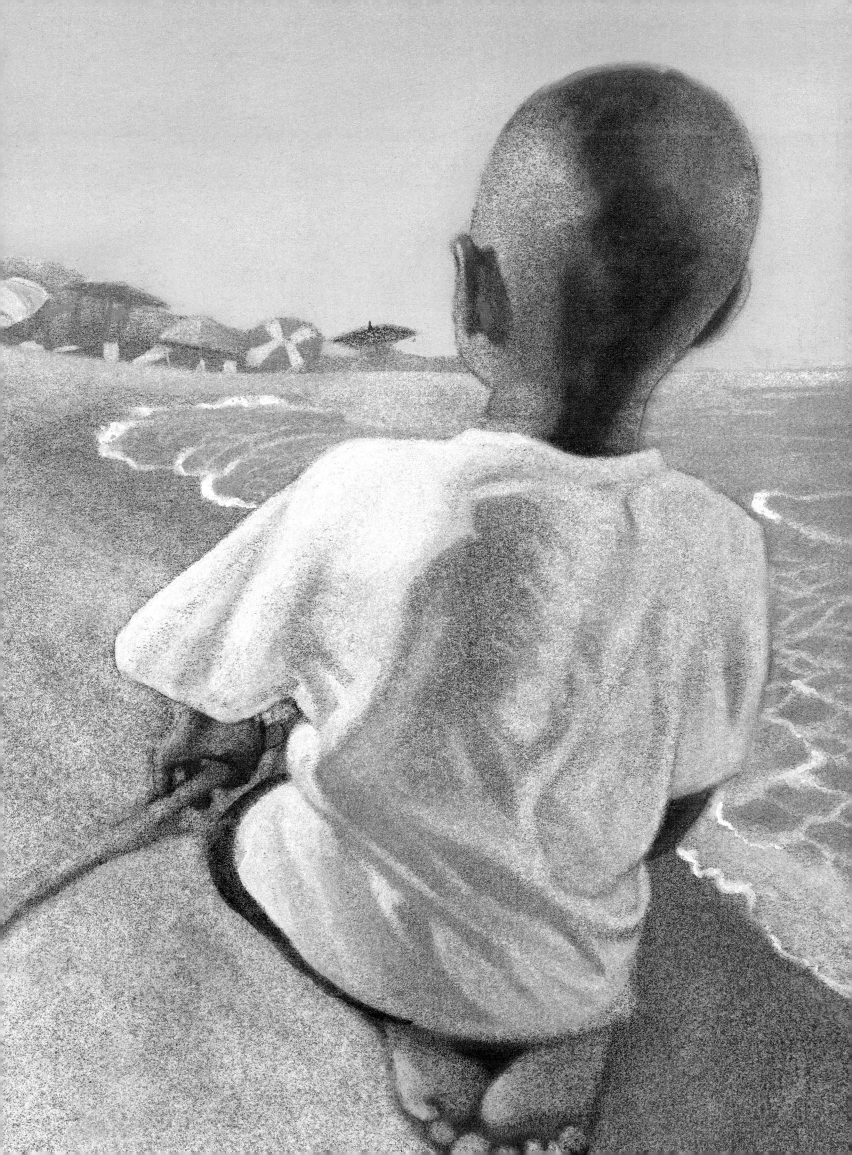

Swish–swoosh

Gregory followed Sandy's tail.
He followed the wavy line.

Swish–swoosh

He traced his nickname backward:
G-E-R-G.
He went around and around
the deep, dark ghost-crab hole.

Swish–swoosh

He went down into the giant hole
and up again.
Zag and then zig.
He went around
the horseshoe crab's pointer.
Uh-oh.
Gregory looked down the beach.
No Sandy.
No Dad on the dolphin towel
under the blue umbrella.
But . . .

Gregory saw the mound
of the old castle
washed smooth by the waves.

Swish–swoosh

He went up and over and down.
There was Sandy's tail
in a loop around the gooey purple jellyfish.

Swish–swoosh

Gregory followed the loop.
And then he came to Sandy.
Uh-oh.

Gregory looked up.
There was the blue umbrella.
There was the dolphin towel.
Dad waved.
"Sandy has a long tail," he said.

"I didn't go in the water,"
Gregory said.
"But Sandy got wet," he added.
Dad held Gregory's hand.
"Let's get wet, too."